PATRICE CHAPLIN is an interna
wright and the author of more tha
most notable works include *Albany*
made into a film starring Jodi Foster and Isabella Rossellini),
Into the Darkness Laughing, *Hidden Star*, *Night Fishing* and
Death Trap. Her stage play *From the Balcony* was com-
missioned by London's National Theatre in conjunction with
Radio 3. As a Bohemian in Paris during the '50s and '60s,
Patrice spent time with Jean-Paul Sartre and Simone de
Beauvoir. Married to Charlie Chaplin's son Michael and liv-
ing and working in Hollywood, she was associated with
Lauren Bacall, Miles Davis, Salvador Dali, Marlon Brando and
Jean Cocteau, who gave her a starring role in one of his films.

In her books *City of Secrets* (2007), *The Portal* (2010) and
The Stone Cradle (2017), Patrice opened the door to entirely
new and compelling elements of the Rennes-le-Château
mystery involving the mysterious Catalan capital of Girona.
The material uncovered resulted in *Lucifer by Moonlight*, the
fallen angel's journey in the modern day.

Patrice is the director of The Bridge, a non-profit organization that leads workshops based in the performing arts as a
new and unique way to help fight addiction. She resides in
North London.

To Janet —

LUCIFER BY MOONLIGHT

A MODERN FABLE

PATRICE CHAPLIN

Illustrated by Melissa Scott-Miller

Love to you
and the little Prince

Patrice
xxx

14·12·17

CLAIRVIEW

Clairview Books Ltd.,
Russet, Sandy Lane,
West Hoathly,
W. Sussex RH19 4QQ

www.clairviewbooks.com

Published in Great Britain in 2017 by Clairview Books

A CIP catalogue record for this book is available from the British Library

Print book ISBN 978 1 905570 91 1
Ebook ISBN 978 1 905570 92 8

Cover by Morgan Creative featuring door image © Sergey
Typeset by DP Photosetting, Neath, West Glamorgan
Printed and bound by 4Edge Ltd, Essex

CONTENTS

DRAMATIS PERSONAE

Lucifer, Lucien, Luc (Lucie Fur)	Fallen Angel
Lucie Fur	Street girl
Ollie	Kentish Town street trader
Olav	Norwegian fashion designer
Penelope Warnby	University student
Professor Warnby	Eminent psychiatrist
Billy Cox	Ex-public schoolboy and entrepreneur
Elysium Fox	Once seen around Thebes; latterly on streets of North London

FOREWORD

Stephen Turoff, the well-established psychic surgeon, finished my treatment and was about to leave the room. I was surprised when he paused. With a full clinic, he usually worked swiftly and always skilfully and pauses were rare. Putting a hand on my shoulder he said, 'An angel is going to visit you in the next two days'. That didn't sound too good. Was I being taken, as one puts it in the healing world, 'over to the other side'?

'Am I going to die?'

Amused, he replied, 'I was just told an angel will visit you. You are not afraid of death?'

He flicked his fingers and laughed. It was no big deal. I tried to look as though I agreed. Stephen does amazing work by channelling surgeons and doctors in spirit, who through him perform the surgery. I have seen amazing results and in my case undeniable progress.

During the following two days I did consider Stephen's prediction and expected the visitation would happen at night. Something would appear in my dream-state. I was relieved when the two days were up. Nothing had happened.

Why didn't I notice that on the second day I had suddenly, out of nowhere, started writing about Lucifer? I was finishing editing my new book, *The Stone Cradle*, ready for publication. This, the account of my mystical journey through Girona, N. E. Spain, focuses on a meteorite crashing to earth millions of years ago — and also a 'being of light', likewise falling from out of space, 5,000 years ago, to the same area on the border of France and Spain.

According to legend, the child was lain on the Stone Cradle. The legend does not specify the child was Lucifer, but that his purpose was to teach and raise our level of consciousness up to the 'etheric', so we could become capable of spiritual experience. The Child of Light, the teacher, walked the earth and opened up the population for healing, to receive wisdom and to develop the higher self. A society was formed to keep this trailing light existent, and continued through the ages to this day.

For centuries, the Stone Cradle has kept its ritual functions and is still used for healing. Does it have power? In its proximity, transformation is evident. The stone is concave from being worn by the bodies of supplicants throughout the ages. They came to recover, to give birth, to die. Salvador Dali said that it existed on 23 dimensions.

What did I know about Lucifer? Alan Parker's memorable movie from 1987, *Angel Heart*. In a First World War song, 'a Lucifer' lit a cigarette. Lucifer was another name for Satan…? From childhood I knew the story of the Garden of Eden and the Fall. Now, I wrote about Lucifer in the modern day, compelled to live without death or rebirth as eternal punishment for the Fall. Present in Kentish Town? Equally, in the Ritz. That was where the inspiration took me. It was a swift experience and afterwards I wondered whether Lucifer is indeed still amongst us.

Now I was faced with the question that has puzzled people for centuries. Is he the dark entity the Church depicts, the Antichrist, or the liberator that some Catalans and Spanish believe gave us freewill? They celebrate his light with rituals, towers, churches, societies and temples to Venus. A Guild of the Shoemakers knew him as Luz and the Celts as Lug. A member of the Society in Catalonia that protects the Cradle told me that 5,521 years ago there began the dawn of the Great Cycle, with the Pleiades on the meridian and the sun preceded by the new morning star, Venus. The being of light was released from Venus on the Spanish side of the frontier. Its purpose? To raise our consciousness to its highest level.

Many creative people today term themselves 'Luciferic'. And why not? Lucifer, restless in the Angelic order, gave man freewill, vision, illusion. Carl Jung was fascinated by Lucifer. As were Madame Blavatsky and the Theosophists. John Milton wrote about Lucifer in 'Paradise Lost'. Rudolf Steiner saw him as the spiritual opposite to Ahriman; intellectual, carrying cultures from Egypt, incarnated in China, visionary. In 1933, Otto Rahn, the German Grail writer, sought the Grail Stone which fell in the Pyrenees mountains from Lucifer's crown, as the rebellious angel fell to earth.

The Church had a different view. Lucifer deflects a light, not his own. Behind it? The void. In the Book of Isaiah, Chapter 14, he is identified as the King of Babylon, conqueror of Jerusalem. Elsewhere he is described as 'the bringer of the morning light'. Lucifer, it is claimed in the Bible, declared, 'I will make myself like the Most High'. And the result: 'He was brought down to the depth of the pit.' 'Those who stare at you, they ponder your fate. Is this the man that made kingdoms tremble?'

And finally, Otto Rahn wrote, 'To open the gates of Lucifer's kingdom you must equip yourself with a skeleton key'.

I went back to Stephen. 'I didn't get the visit from an angel.'

'Oh, really?' He paused. 'What are you doing now? Writing? What about?'

I paused. 'Of course, Lucifer was an angel.'

'An archangel.' He started out of the door and turned to me. 'The Light Bringer.'

Patrice Chaplin, June 2017

PROLOGUE

The old child in his cradle, still known as the Light Bringer, is up to his tricks, dazzling his followers, seemingly filled with brilliance but in truth deflecting light; for he has no light. He lies rocking on the stone, absorbing beams from the moon which in turn takes his reflection for payment, his identity to be used in some future century when the tricky one again runs short and light is scarce. The moon, uncaring, fills him up like a pump at a petrol station. The old fraud, with his dyed red hair, waits helpless on the stone for a female to pass so he can be born again and, almost human, strut along the city streets, stealing light from even the meanest doorway. 'And they all fall for it', he concludes, 'after all these years they've not learned a thing.'

1970, LONDON

Lucie Fur by Moonlight, Kentish Town

Lucie Fur the street girl, her prices 'high as the moon',
chucked in a smoke as an extra, depending on her mood.
'High as the moon you say?' Her laugh was disconcerting.
'That uncaring bauble, no friend of yours or mine. Not even
well known. As far as this galaxy is concerned, it's definitely
out in the suburbs. It's a fake. Steals its light from the sun.

Want a smoke?' Her voice was rough and, it was said on the street, this boy-girl 'kicked with both feet'.

The boy said she was so clever. 'Some say you're an old soul.'

'Old soul!' She couldn't laugh enough. She wrapped her attractiveness out of sight in the ocelot fur, not allowing even a small gap for enticement. She liked her furs and the local guys couldn't get how she acquired them. Someone had said she lay on a tombstone in Highgate cemetery. Is that where she earned the furs?

'You're only a working girl.'

'Correction,' said Lucie, 'I'm a harlot.'

The boy had never heard the word and, having no dictionary at home, had to go to the library to look it up.

Lucie Fur crept along by the light of the moon. This was one long night. Then she saw the worst thing. The fox padded on the other side of the street, looking for what it thought it wanted but didn't get. It ate some rubbish. And then it saw Lucie Fur. 'Worst case scenario.' She hoped the modern lingo would distract the creature. It crossed the street and smelt her legs. Something was wrong.

'I've seen you before.'

'Oh shut it, you dumb rodent', said Lucie. 'We go back years and more years. I last saw you in Thebes.'

'Don't you get tired of not getting old?' The fox even sounded tricky. He licked the fur coat. 'Nice fur, but its last owner died in it.' Then it took a snap at her leg and broke the strap of her Ferragamo shoe.

'You'll pay for that, you vermin', she said. And the electric shock from her skin cost the fox the loss of some teeth. And she clattered off on the broken shoe. 'See you around, Fox. Some century or other.'

2010, LONDON

Dole Queue, Kentish Town

The dole queue was longer than a queue for a hit movie when Lucifer arrived one depressed winter morning. He did not like waiting, and turned a fragment of stone around in his hand. It was a piece from the Stone Cradle and he waited for it to calm him. His hair was slicked up in scarlet points; eyes long and green in his girlish face. He carried a violin case.

'What made your hair stick up like that?' said Mick the Tick. 'Electric shock?' He considered kicking the case but as he said later, something about the red-haired geezer stopped him and he didn't know what.

Ollie dragged his way through the queue and the group gave

him pavement space. He had been a known villain and got respect. He pointed at Lucifer's case. 'What you got in there?'

'A violin, of course.'

'Trying to sell it?'

'Learning to play it.'

Guys nearby laughed mockingly. Ollie turned, snarling, worse than a pit bull terrier, and all laughter ceased. Ollie squinted at an official paper. 'Bad news, Lucifer. Got the doctor's report. I've only got two months.'

'What? Dole money?'

'To live.'

'You lucky bastard. I've got 2,000 years.'

Ollie nudged him: 'And no more carrying that violin thing around here, it gives me a bad name.'

Cemetery, Highgate

Lucifer lay on the tombstone in Highgate Cemetery. He'd dressed up for the occasion in a green ribbed, three-piece suit. His long earring fitted perfectly against the rough stone. Ollie, overweight and falling apart, sat on the neighbouring grave.

'I'll be lying in one of these soon enough.'

Lucifer was gazing at the sky. 'I used to lie on a stone like this, except it rocked. And I watched the moon all night.'

Ollie asked about the Cradle.

'A Cradle through which spirits have to pass to be born here. It's made of stone from a falling meteorite', Lucifer said.

What kind of gear was this one on? It really puzzled Ollie.

'I'll go to my death confused. I'll die trying to work out what you're taking.'

Lucifer lay back silent on the tombstone. He was trying to absorb death.

Cinema, Camden

Lucifer laughed through most of the showing of the movie *The Exorcist* until the audience, outraged, finally got him thrown out. This said quite a lot for his inappropriate laughter, seeing as it was a rough cinema in the worst part of Camden and you had to be quite something to get chucked out of there.

Lucifer picked himself up out of the gutter and Ollie offered to brush him down. He thought Lucifer's reaction to movies was seriously out of order. He laughed at the demonic horror of *The Exorcist*, sneered at Damien in *The Omen* yet cried all the way through *Bambi*.

'I hate lies', said Lucifer. 'Especially when they lie about me.'

'You lost me there', said Ollie.

'All that satanic bullshit. That dodgy priest. I thought it was a comedy.'

'I'm lost.' Ollie offered him a smoke. 'It's an old film. It's nothing.'

'I also discover I am mentioned only once by name in the Bible. It's been a bad day.'

Ollie shivered. 'I don't like it when you talk like that. It's creepy. You're just an ordinary dude.' And Ollie realized that was the last thing he was.

Lucifer turned on him. 'I tell you what, Mr Extraordinary. Why don't you go home and read through the Bible, every page, and write down how many times you see my name. L-U-C-I-F-E-R.' He over-pronounced each letter. 'Got it?'

'I'm not sure I've got that book right now.'

'Then go in a church and nick one – and remember, I don't like lies. These lousy movies make me out to be some sicko loser. I thought that last one was a comedy. I was big. Do you understand? I was at the top table.'

'I think so', said Ollie now nervous. 'I'll go and find a Bible but I think they keep all the churches locked these days.'

'You bet they do', said Lucifer, suddenly pleased.

1999, NORWAY

Oslo

Olav had always been the furrier to go to. Even the Queen chose his designs. He had brought out the best in all the divas, even dressed Dietrich on her deathbed and the broken-hearted Greek for her own funeral. He'd learned his trade in Paris in the best years, with Balenciaga and Dior. He used to make up Dior's tender little black dresses with a touch of white for the Belle Rive set that used to gamble and dance in Deauville.

Olav always accompanied a fashionable wealthy woman, usually married, on her travels around the world, and dressed her accordingly. He made money, he spent money, he was given enough, and then in 1993 he suddenly went broke. Fur was not in fashion. His dresses were condemned as old-fashioned. He was, he said, holding back age with both hands. He tried to write a biography – after all, he had met everyone. Opening a boutique failed. He was usually on the wrong side of his morning vodkas and went downhill from then on. In debt, he hocked his chandeliers, his memorabilia, had gone on the dole and struggled to pay rent. And then suddenly, in May 1999, he came into a substantial sum of money.

His friends believed it was a bequest. Marvin, the actor, assumed he would go straight to the broker and get back his array of valuable jewellery. He had long been mourning his $150,000 watch. It was irreplaceable. Yet on the morning of the windfall, he sped straight across town to the cold storage of a little-known furrier and demanded back his assortment of furs that were rarely mentioned. The actor Marvin knew only that the furs had been placed in cold storage, 'to keep their integrity'. Some real classy sable and ocelot. Marvin recalled later how Olav had swanned into the shop with his usual high-end attitude and the furrier had turned pale. At first he said he didn't recognize Olav, who promptly presented a receipt in a plastic cover. When the furrier glanced at the list of items, he became even paler.

'But this is over six years ago. You put them into my storage in 1993 and you only paid, as I remember, for two or three months.' The furrier looked up the details and recovered his colour. 'Yes', he said. 'You haven't paid for six years.'

'Well I'm paying now. Cash.' And Olav put a pile of notes on the counter. 'First, I'd like to check the condition of my furs.'

The man returned to his screen to gain time and his jaw whipped to and fro as though recapturing escaping false teeth. 'They're gone.'

'Gone!' It was Olav's turn to become pale.

The man, more sure of himself now, said that, as they had not been paid for, he had not been able to keep them in his cold storage and had tried every way to reach Olav who, it seemed, had changed his phone number and address. And finally, only a month or two ago, he had reluctantly put them up for sale.

'But you have no right to sell items put into your care.'

'Six years?' said the man, and his jaw clamped shut.

'Six years or sixty', said Olav. 'We'll see what my lawyer says about this.' He started for the door, his well-kept skin turning from white to strong pink. Then he looked back at the furrier and made sure they met eye to eye. 'You couldn't have done a worse thing. If only you knew who those furs belong to!'

Outside the shop, Marvin tried to placate his friend. 'He probably did try to reach you.' Olav, as everyone in smart Oslo knew, was on the run and had moved frequently due to rent owed.

'It's who they belonged to.' Olav sounded matter-of-fact.

'The Queen?' Marvin's voice was soft.

'Oh, much worse.'

Olav went back into the shop and asked to whom the furs had been sold.

The furrier didn't bother with the screen. 'A good customer of mine wanted the sable.'

'I bet he did', said Olav.

'So he took the lot as a bulk sale.' The man couldn't remember the exact price.

'Let's see if you do better remembering his name?'

'It wouldn't help.' The man opened his arms in submission. 'They were stolen.'

Olav paused for only the smallest moment. 'They sure stole the wrong fur.' And, decisively, he – with Marvin following – left the furrier to make what he would out of that threat.

* * *

The lost furs made Olav desperate but his friends tried to cheer him up. It was a lot of money, they agreed, but he had lived without them for over six years. His reply was always the same. 'You don't know who they belonged to.'

'Don't tell me it's the Princess', said his best friend, the most famous actress in Scandinavia.

'If only.'

'That would be bad enough', she said. 'Anyone I know? The divas are all dead.'

He almost told her the truth. But Lucifer lived in a shady world of secrets and could be anywhere. The actress offered to send a serious man to talk to the furrier. What she meant was: alpha male, tough and effective.

'Let's find out who he sold them to and a little more detail on this robbery. Also, you need a lawyer.' She considered giving him some financial aid then remembered that these days he didn't need it.

'You're doing better now. I hear you're back in the chips.'

Having the money did not cheer Olav. Then he noticed his clock. The hands were going backwards. That always happened when Lucifer was nearby. He got the actress out and waited, prepared to die.

1989, NORWAY

Oslo

Lucie Fur got her sable coats, stoles and fur-lined ponchos from Olav. She used to ply her trade in the area near the Theatre Café or down by the fjord in Acke Brugge. Then, one day in the early 1990s, when she visited Olav in his apartment in Trump Tower, New York, he discovered she was not female. Olav was in heaven. That was the only way he could put it.

'Heaven? Not there!' said Lucifer scraping off his wig.

Olav took him to the clubs and introduced him to the stars and the powerful. He adored him utterly but never got him to bed.

'Let's call me Luc', said Lucifer, right from the start. 'It'll be easier with these sorts of people.'

Back in Norway, they stayed together but Luc was always going out. Olav never knew where or when he'd return. He told Marvin, the actor, it was ruining his health and his ability to work. Luc loved his designs. He especially loved the furs. He liked to lie on Olav's chaise lounge and listen to Bach. But underneath he was restless. One day he said he needed to go to the big city.

'But this is it', said Olav.

'No. I mean big. This place is the suburbs.'

'Oslo?'

'The planet.' Luc got up, laughing, and threw Olav his sable. 'Look after it for me. And all my furs. I'll be back.'

It was after Luc left in 1993 that Olav started drinking and the money ran out. He put the furs in the safest place he could and at first tried very hard to find the money for the payments. He never did.

1999, NORWAY

Oslo

Leaving his flat for the dole queue, Olav found a bundle of money in a large carrier bag outside his door. Being in a fairly dubious block, he thought it was stolen money, dropped on the stairwell by tenants chased by police. It had to be from a substantial robbery, but nothing was reported in the news. And then Olav looked properly at the large carrier bag. The company was called simply: 'The Light Bringer'. The letters were bright gold. In one corner, a crescent moon. Olav reconsidered his luck. Not necessarily good. And then the hands on his clock started going the wrong way. So the first thing Olav did was to speedily redeem the furs for Lucifer, as the money had probably come from him. Did he know they were in storage? Without any doubt, he would come to reclaim them.

After the appalling news that the furs were stolen, Olav tried to recover his nerves enough to get himself to the dole office the following week. His friend the actress had sent an investigator to the downtown shop. The furrier's story did not fit too well, not if you were looking for 'plausible'. 'You leave too many holes', said the investigator. 'Does this unfortunate new purchaser who was robbed have a name, and were the police called? How much did you make on the deal?'

The furrier could only spread his arms in submission. He was doing a lot of that these days.

'You are the thief', the investigator decided. 'You sold them for your own gain, probably years ago.'

'If only it could be that way.' The furrier sounded regretful.

The investigator suggested he try telling the truth. Better still, get the furs back. The furrier said it might be possible but would take a few hours. The investigator gave him just two. When he came back later in the day, the shop was closed for the foreseeable future and the furrier was gone.

The dole queue was long and Olav disliked the unkempt, ill-sorted selection of human beings on their uppers and dreaded any proximity. Then one had the effrontery to touch him on the shoulder and Olav turned, ready with scorching abuse. But then he saw the hand. It did not belong in this queue and he knew that ring, its snake design curled in heavy silver and diamonds.

'What's a pretty boy like you doing in this place?' said Lucifer.

Olav grimaced and tried for sympathy. 'They want me to go for an emergency medical. They didn't believe I was sick and now they do. Only too well.' He hoped that he was pale enough.

'It's funny', said Lucifer. 'I always seem to end up in dole queues with guys who aren't going to make it. It's always bad news. Even for me. I've got another 2,000 years.'

Olav didn't get that one.

'To live.'

Lucifer nearly lost his composure. 'This lot here have months or even a year left. They don't know how lucky they are.'

Olav, for once lost without an answer, understood Luc

wasn't just a flyweight street boy with a dangerous edge. He was something else altogether. Olav tried for sympathy.

'Don't make fun of life. I only have a few weeks at this rate.'

'What are you dying from?'

'After a terrible burglary – which I knew nothing about and that's the truth – I collapsed in the street. It made me ill with stress.'

'You don't die from stress, you die from lack of breath.' Lucifer laughed, a rare sound in this queue. 'And don't worry about any burglary. You could call it divine intervention; a just reclaiming of what is mine.'

Oh God, thought Olav. What is this new horror? 'But they were stolen.'

'That's as maybe. But I can trace my furs by their perfume. I had a little trouble persuading the would-be new owner they weren't his sort of thing. People are sometimes frightened of

me, so getting them back was not a problem. But the man then became offensive. That was the problem.'

'He's alive?'

'Certainly', said Lucifer. 'Somewhere.'

Olav expected 'somewhere' did not include 'here' and burst into tears. 'I've even used stolen money to buy food. It gets worse.'

Lucifer was comforting and almost stroked the ageing hair.

'Legit money. I left it for you. I heard you were broke.'

'You're an angel.'

'Oh be careful with that word. All in the past, I'm afraid.'

'I'll pay it back', said Olav recklessly.

'It's only money. Nothing to worry about. But I wanted my furs.'

'I did my best.' Olav knew he'd never done his best and promised again he would stop drinking.

'Your furs are like no other. I will always wear them.' And Lucifer realized that, for him, 'always' was a harsh word.

2017, LONDON

Gloucester Place

Today, Lucifer will hear his story in the Palisades, a substantial 1860s building devoted to the development of 'human understanding'.

Lucifer, riding around on the Circle line tube, reading his favourite ever book – *Against Nature* by J. K. Huysmans – knew the passages he loved by heart. 'Charles, I used to call him Charlie, was a true purveyor of decadence.' He realized he had spoken aloud.

By chance, the student on the next seat to his, a girl in her early 20s, knew the book and decided to challenge the veracity of his remark. Glancing at the cover she said, 'Huysmans lived in the 19th century, so how could you know him?' She looked at Lucifer more closely. He had seemed young, but there was an assessing watchfulness in his expression that could only come from experience.

Lucifer, normally never at a loss, found himself stuck between two answers. The first was a prompt and discouraging reply; the second, one of curiosity. Choosing the second, he asked if reading *Against Nature* had changed her thinking. She had long, dark curly hair and beautiful bone structure and skin; no thanks to her, it was all inherited.

'It made me want to read it again. It became an experience that was an active part of me.'

Lucifer liked the answer. He decided she had an academic father she looked up to, and of course there would be a brother, younger and spoilt. He asked about her education – the minimum – and her answers were to be expected. She added she was also a student at the Palisades, founded by J. C. Irving, the discoverer and philanthropist. One of his centres was nearby in Gloucester Place. 'J. C. trekked across the Himalayas to the Far East in the '20s and '30s and brought back Mindfulness. You must have heard of him.' Lucifer had not.

She gave him a pamphlet with the Palisades' forthcoming programme, then got up as the train slowed.

'Huysmans' name was Charles', said Lucifer, quite offhand.

She laughed and he liked her youthfulness. 'You sound as though you could have known him.'

She was gone and he turned the pages of the pamphlet, in which a surprise was waiting. He was the focus of a full page advert. 'Evening With Lucifer. The Palisades, 7.30 pm.'

That was one evening he would not miss.

* * *

The speaker was solid on her stuff and spoke a sturdy English, middle-class posh, that would silence some schoolchildren and all husbands. Elsie Mayhew had been lecturing on J. C. Irving since the 1960s and had a small loyal following of slightly shabby, musty leftover figures from the 1950s. A lot of darned socks and patched jackets in this room. Lucifer, easily the star of the evening, wearing a silk-lined Olav suit, sat near the door. The twenty-three assembled followers smelt of tobacco, old Woolworths' lavender water, cheap cleaning products, traces of Yardley's soap, and dust – as though a multitude of Hoovers had been recently emptied in their midst. He had rarely seen such an odd bunch. How had they got together? Having an acute sense of smell, Lucifer found the assembly nauseous and asked for a window – which had not been used for years – to be opened, in order to allow in a little Central London air. There followed a communal shiver and protest and the window was firmly shut. He was given a cup of tea, railway station quality *circa* 1951, with the obligatory overdose of milk.

Elsie Mayhew's discourse covered J. C. Irving's history of matter. She described earth energies, previous ancient planetary incarnations, the soul state and the effect of gravity. She was doing alright, he decided, as long as one wasn't expecting to hear the truth. And then she mentioned Venus and its part in the progression of matter. Venus was not a cheap women's magazine horoscope-vehicle that brought in the passage of love, sex and luck. It was, rather, his true home. And, loyal to his longed-for place of residence from which he had been denied, he accused her of slander and lies. The audience hoped his brief interruption would settle down and they turned again to the speaker. 'I will deal with your objection later', she said. Her eyes glittered. She did not like Lucifer.

The planet had, according to J. C. Irving, passed through a variety of conditions – air, heat, pure spirit, water, angelic influence, the goddesses – and then she said: 'We now come to an examination of Lucifer'. She explained he was an archangel, restless in the midst of angelic obedience, that was blessed but not with choice. He rebelled and gave mankind the opportunity to think for themselves and, in return, caused 'the Fall'. This archangel, loved by God, was promptly flung from Paradise and brought limitless destruction and darkness. But Lucifer, she suggested, had opened the minds of

men. The Bible gave him a bad time. J. C. Irving stated that
Lucifer brought light, choice, daring. Many of today's artists
and musicians, influenced by light and free thought, termed
themselves Luciferic. Through the ages, Lucifer was mistaken
for Satan. That figure of darkness was, in J. C. Irving's world,
'the Antichrist'. Ms Mayhew ended on a crescendo of ignor-
ance, in Lucifer's opinion, and said the falling archangel was
good and had wanted the best for mankind. When he was in
the Sun State, billions of years' past, he was the 'brother' of
Jesus. And that was the truth about Lucifer. After a respectful
silence, the audience was invited to ask questions.

Was it seeing an engraving of himself on the wall that made
Lucifer laugh uncontrollably? Usually, pictures of him
included huge wings, webbed feet, sometimes a tail.

'I wouldn't be caught dead looking like that', he said,
pointing to the wall.

Before Ms Mayhew could turn nasty, he changed his tone.
Soft and cunning, he asked where Lucifer was today. 'Still
falling?'

'Sinking fast into darkness, causing trouble. His redemp-
tion is only foreseeable when he returns to the Ancient Sun
State with his brother.'

Was it the mention of Jesus on the Sun that brought out his
terrible mockery. Standing up, he said: 'Lucifer may be
sinking alright but what about this room? It's low enough.
Why, he could even be you, Ms Mayhew. That out-of-control,
undernourished grey hair of yours, with its cheap yellow tint,
could hide a lot of things. Even a devil's horn...'

'But Lucifer represents good!' she said, her face scarlet.
'Don't you understand?'

'Lucifer is condemned to eternal existence. You are doing

nothing but harm to his image. I wouldn't have you as my P.R.'

The group turned on him in no uncertain way. He assured them, in return, that this ridiculous spinster belonged back in the 1960s, her teaching acumen at the level of a *Reader's Digest* magazine. She knew nothing of Lucifer; the being trailed energies she could never imagine. The only thing these people had in common with the former archangel was that they, the group, were out of time. Where could they reside but in this dowdy, effete and unclean meeting house? He would have caused more trouble, but several men got up and asked him to leave. He could never leave a scene like this, and couldn't wait for it to become really chaotic. It took five of the antiquated men and one slim guard to escort the former archangel down in the 1920s lift and throw him out onto the wide clean pavement opposite the Royal park.

The student from the Circle line was suddenly beside him, helping him up. He had better make haste because the men were calling the police.

'Oh, it gets even better' – and he brushed the street dirt from Olav's creation, made in honour of his undying love for the archangel.

'What did you want to say all that for?'

He let her lead him across the road to the Chinese restaurant and he realized she'd been in the audience, although he had not seen her. He liked the look of the restaurant. He liked its smell.

'Can't you see that Lucifer is misunderstood?'

'Definitely', he said.

'Ms Mayhew knows him inside and out.'

'Not a chance.' And he took her into the restaurant and

bought her a satisfactory dinner. Penelope Warnby, 21, wanting only the best results in life, fell in love with the former archangel between the assorted dumplings and lucky dip mottoes. She said later it was his laugh that did it.

They left in good spirits to be met by a delegation from the Palisades. Ms Mayhew was pressing charges. A policeman crossed the road and asked for Lucifer's name and address.

'Lucifer. The Dole Queue. Kentish Town.'

The policeman warned him: another remark like that and he would be booked.

The student spoke up promptly. 'I will look after him. He's not been well lately. I will get him some help.' She reached for her mobile phone. 'I will get my uncle now.' Her uncle, Professor Warnby, celebrated psychiatrist, was known to the J. C. Irving group. The student was well-connected, her family influential, and it was agreed she would take the misguided visitor to her uncle's apartment straight away.

The Palisades wanted some indication of what then transpired as Ms Mayhew was intent on pressing charges. Penelope Warnby cut in brusquely and reminded the small group that the policy of J. C. was to heal and mend, to seek the best result for the common good.

'Is this man willing to talk to a psychiatrist?' the policeman asked.

Lucifer seemed to consider the matter. There was nothing wrong with it but he would prefer to go out and listen to music.

'You may as well. Talk to him.' Penelope encouraged him into the taxi. 'They mean business and my uncle is a better option than a police cell.'

'I may as well indeed', he said. 'I like the ridiculous. I hope he's a Jungian.'

'Eclectic', and the cab went south to Belgravia.

'What is your name by the way?' Penelope asked.

'Lucifer.'

'Please don't start that again.'

'Luc, spelt the French way.' He considered stopping the taxi and going to his old club off Belgrave Square, but the idea of a session with a psychiatrist added to the night's drama, which on the whole he had enjoyed.

Prof.'s Study

The room was pleasant, a log fire lit, a tray of coffee together with the Professor's favourite biscuits already waiting on the side table. Penelope and Lucifer sat together on a sofa and she couldn't stop prompting him: 'Tell him you have moments of delusion.'

Lucifer wasn't keen on that. He was either delusional or not. He didn't like the idea of 'moments'.

'You said you knew the author Huysmans who has been dead for years. You suffer from hallucinations. I can be a witness to that.'

Professor Warnby came gently into the room, a little bowed and with substantial bushy eyebrows and crinkled wayward hair that reached out electrically in all directions. His eyes were concentrated, far seeing and didn't miss much. His navy blue pin-striped suit had had the attention of several women – brushing, flattening, straightening, dabbing – but all their efforts fell away to nothing the moment 'the Prof.', as he was called, got himself inside it. Today the waistcoat was grey with droppings of cigarette ash, the obligatory handkerchief, visible and unwanted, in the wrong pocket. Lucifer approved of him immediately and got up eagerly from the sofa to shake his hand. Penelope called him Prof. He called his niece Penny. 'Pour the coffee. There's a good girl. Don't forget the brandy.'

He sat in the comfortable chair by the fire and indicated that Lucifer sit opposite. This chair was more demanding, upright and resistant; its padded seat thin, legs spindly. 'French 1830s', he said, rubbing the unfriendly arms. 'I used to think sitting on one of these was like trying to take the virginity of an ageing spinster.'

The Professor, eyes sparkling now, was amused. His niece was unsure about giving Lucifer brandy. 'He may be on meds.'

'He'll decide that.' And Prof. sipped his drink with satisfaction.

The carriage clock ticked loudly. When Lucifer was around, clocks behaved unusually. Lucifer, who disliked common mood-changing substances, pushed the brandy glass to one side. The Prof. leaned forward.

'So, who have I the pleasure of speaking to?'

'I am Lucifer.'

'Of course you are.' The Professor stoked the fire. 'So what brings you here?'

'Your lovely niece.'

Of course, the Professor did not believe him. 'And a spot of trouble outside the Palisades. What's that restaurant like by the way?'

'Much better than I expected.'

'Why didn't you walk out during that talk?'

'I was insulted. The discrepancies in my story were unforgivable.'

'Couldn't you just have gone?'

'The woman irritated me, talking about the sun and Jesus and me somewhere on it. Too much!'

'I think you're referring to Irving's Ancient Sun.'

'I am Lucifer. I am here for the duration.' He knew this man did not believe him. No one would. Except another lunatic. If he insisted on his identity, he would be condemned as mad. He could see the Professor was preparing for some deceptive procedure. 'I knew Jung.' He sounded offhand. 'I had the pleasure of talking to him.'

'So why are you talking to me?'

'I had to tell someone.'

'About?'

'The way to get through it all.'

'You are out of the box. There's the problem. No one will listen to you. However marvellous your reality has been. So get back in the box and fit in and you won't have to keep proving yourself.'

Penelope was losing. Lucifer would not get help. She said he was talking to people from years ago. 'He's hallucinating.'

'Don't diagnose him.'

The Professor sounded sharp. She retaliated. They almost started quarrelling. If only they did. Lucifer was excited. But good manners prevailed and she withdrew into silence.

This place had no help for Lucifer so he got out of the chair, saying goodnight.

'You have to be in the box and stay away from the Palisades and those sort of places', said Prof.

Lucifer thanked him and went out into the night in search of Ollie.

* * *

The Prof. realized his niece was upset — but worse — had fallen for the man. That was how he saw him. A man. She saw him as an enchanting youth, bringing light and laughter into her world. Prof. wasn't sure about the laughter. He agreed that the recent visitor chose not to reveal fear.

'He has no fear', she corrected him. 'He comes from the edge. That's where you'll find him. He will do anything. Charming, erudite, creative. He puts the lights on in the shadows. I am sure he is a painter, using old signs that are new to us. He knows the world. Utterly sure of himself. But that's the class. He was born with that.'

Prof. reached for the brandy bottle. 'Definitely Eton. I wonder who his mother was.'

'Real class. He has grace', Penelope decided wistfully. 'He makes me feel alive.'

Her uncle hoped his skills as a psychiatrist would not be too tested in this situation, which he had first surmised as 'a little family matter'. Penelope could see her uncle wasn't quite as taken with him as she was.

'No good as a partner. Comes and goes. Breaks hearts. It's all to do with the mother.' It occurred to him the man was hard as a rock.

'Of course he comes and goes', she said. 'He's sought after. His class is always there and saves him.'

Hard as a rock. And Prof. stroked her childlike hand, glad she was safe.

2017, NORWAY

Oslo

On some nights, Olav sensed Lucifer calling to him and he'd go out into the streets of Oslo and then end up in the bars and clubs, on the edge of disgrace or sometimes danger. Had anyone seen Lucifer? Occasionally, a man or two had news of Lucie Fur and heard she was back, busy around the uptown hotels, draped in ocelot or sable. Olav, even when drunk, found that unlikely, as he was master of the furs.

Chantal, the divine model, from the '60s, a photo of her by Helmut Newton on offer for 70K, used to dance with Luc in Studio 54, NY. She thought it was 1964. It could not be the same person. Did Lucifer look that old?

'What's time?' said Chantal. In her case, everything. Only surgery held the worst at bay. She hinted she had slept with Luc. Olav put that down to drink and one-upmanship. But he still said he would let Chantal wear one of Luc's furs for a day if she recalled that night, so long ago. Chantal declined the offer but accepted another hard liquor, Aquavit. 'Can't remember much, but there was one thing. He didn't have a belly button.'

Olav was confused for only a moment. 'He must have had a navel; after all, he has gone through being born and you need an umbilical cord for that. He just had the traces removed by plastic surgery.'

Chantal asked why.

'Obviously wanted to appear naked and unmarked.' Olav

remembered how Lucifer liked smooth skin and good flesh. And then his own remark about being born demanded attention.

'Did you get anything on his mother?'

'Lucifer was a class act', she said. 'I get the sense she was French and real aristocracy, going back centuries. And that she was hard as…

She nearly added 'nails' but chose 'stone'.

Olav dragged his weight, sodden with many drinks, back to his small flat, and the drink made the chandeliers swing. He decided it was so hard being human. All upkeep, defying age, fearing poverty, losing everything, and he realized – with some surprise – that Lucifer didn't go through that.

Women talked about Luc. How lucky not to fall for him. What made him so attractive, so charismatic? At least two women had killed themselves because of him. The mercifully unaffected ones said they found him cold. An artist in the 1970s had spent one night with him – a night she had never got over. She said, before she jumped from the roof, that she was blessed to have had that night and life was too grey in comparison.

In his own files, Prof. had found details of a woman that Lucifer had stayed with in NY in the 1980s. The woman's sister had been Prof.'s client and had recounted the story. 'He went under the name of Lucien and was sought after by NY's social set. After some weeks he packed his bags suddenly, and I remember my sister telling him that if he left she'd rather be dead. And he said, "lucky you"! I disliked him from the start'.

Prof. asked if the sister had money.

'Of course. You'd never see him with a poor one.'

2017, LONDON

The Palisades

Ollie watched as Lucifer painted the wall in red and black, the sweeping brush strokes too loud for the quiet night. 'If a rozzer comes past, you're done. You're no Banksy and this ain't Camden Town.'

The building was large, sturdy, secure and had a righteous atmosphere – its walls absent, so far, of graffiti. This place belonged to a more innocent time. Lucifer was up above the portal of the main door, balanced on a window ledge, legs astride, brush held high. Ollie reached up with more paint. Under the huge winged figure dripped the message: 'Lucifer For Good'.

'Hey ho – devil's colours: red and black', said Ollie. 'D'you mean he's good, or here for good?'

'What do you think?' The way he answered didn't give much choice.

The next day people passing the Palisades got quite a surprise.

Prof.'s Study

'You thought I'd come by', Lucifer told Prof. as he looked for somewhere to place the flowers.

'We'll give them to Annie. I'm no good at this kind of thing.' And Prof. called for the housekeeper. 'So you're still out of the box', he told Lucifer.

'But you still let me in.' He waited for Prof. to settle in his chair. 'I thought your niece might like orchids. You don't get that kind much this time of year. No artificial smell in those. They are the real thing.'

The Prof. waited for him to continue. Lucifer looked at the carriage clock. It was behaving normally. Then he looked at the Prof., his eyes solemn. 'When you say box, do you mean a coffin?'

Prof. nodded. 'That might be the answer. It is, after all, the end. For most people.'

'I'm sorry about the Palisades because I don't want to hurt your niece. She was kind to me. I like her. I hope the flowers will go some way to atone.'

'Oh, I won't give them to her. I think we'll leave her out of this. That would be the best recompense. Why are you really here?'

'Ms Mayhew gave me an idea. Why shouldn't Lucifer be good? He's been misunderstood all these years.'

'In the third person today.' The Prof. paused. He had done enough pausing in his life in order to do it well. When he had the visitor's fullest attention, he asked his question: 'What do you do for a living?'

'A bit of this and that. Mostly clock watching like everyone else.' He changed the way his legs were crossed and the movement had a certain danger. His green eyes were alight and ready for trouble, all instinctive.

'You don't like direct questions', said the Prof., matter of fact.

'Do for a living? Why don't you ask me what I do for a dying?'

'You have a touch of vulgarity in your tone. It's something

you've picked up from mixing with rough Londoners. Perhaps common people', said Prof. thoughtfully.

'I hope so', said Lucifer. 'I like common people. I'm vulgar for the sake of it.'

'Who was your mother?'

'The Countess de Montmorency', he replied without pause.

'Difficult', said Prof. 'Sounds like a character from Proust's *Remembrance of Things Past*.

'Not so', replied Lucifer swiftly. 'The Princess of Parma was the character based on my mother, Countess de Montmorency.'

'So why are you here?'

'I suppose I need someone to talk to.' He changed direction sharply. 'What do people do when they are at their end?'

'Kill time.'

Lucifer liked that.

'They go to church if they're really at their end.'

Lucifer got up. 'I'm sorry about the Palisades. That meeting did one thing. They think he's good so I might as well be good. Hence, Lucifer for good.'

'People think Lucifer is a figment of the collective imagination.'

'We will see.' And he went to the door with his soft walk.

Holland Park

Lucifer pulled strings and his smart friends – who knew him from Eton as Lucien de Montmorency – put on an evening of 'Luciferic Influences in the Modern World'. The banker's Holland Park house held fifty guests comfortably, and afterwards they repaired to the Firehouse in Chiltern Street for a decent dinner and enough space for discussion.

They all agreed Lucien was 'damn good at history' and 'brought it to life'. He should have done a Masters at Oxford instead of excavation in northern Spain. One or two of the group had never really 'got' Lucien. He was a wild card. Others decided he was a 'bit of a magician' but 'nothing wrong in that'. He was, in fact, a devil at cards and some said that was how he made his money, although it was known he had an inheritance. He spoke well at the Holland Park evening and discussed the true nature of the one who had given man freedom of choice, caused the Fall and paid forever afterwards. The being was 'a teacher'. He came from the Highest. He opened the Door of the Morning.

His audience agreed his light influenced creative people who became Luciferic, and that the bad operator was Satan. Those belonging to the church disagreed and said Lucifer did not give light but deflected a light that was not his own and was blinded by his own charisma. But what was behind his light? That was the question. The churchgoers knew the answer. Nothing.

Lucifer had suddenly become popular. Graffiti that read 'Lucifer For Good' was spreading over London and became an underground phenomenon. The popular band Take Me had a number one hit with 'Make Me Good, I'm Misunderstood'. Lucien actually preferred the '60s song, 'Angel of the Morning'. It was his favourite of those composed for him.

The banker was aroused by the flurry of success. A business proposal had been made to him to promote Lucifer with bracelets, badges, pentagram jewellery, 'mind openers' and other trivia.

The happening at the Firehouse was the talk of the group for weeks afterwards. Billy Cox remarked that Lucien never seemed to age. The others were amazed that they hadn't noticed. What was he on?

'I look after myself', Lucien replied, his voice low and without colour.

'Meditation and that sort of thing?' asked the banker, who recently started yoga to keep age at bay.

'It's the Montmorency genes', decided one of his dorm. mates from Eton.

Lucifer was exasperated. How could he let this happen? Why had he steeped himself in the sloth of Kentish Town dole queues and not looked in a mirror. At least a touch of shadow under his eyes, a streak of grey, different teeth. Most of the men at the table had those run-of-the-mill ice-white implants and bridges. Billy Cox then said his PA had asked what Lucien's secret was.

'So what's it all about?' said the banker. 'Another Dorian Gray?' The men laughed; an unpleasant neighing sound.

Lucifer put on tinted glasses and complained of a sudden headache. Monotonously, he said he didn't drink or smoke and chose a vegan way of life. 'I bathe in the morning light.' What was he saying? Was he mad? He said he would go home shortly. He said he was tired. He sounded tired. He also sounded as though he was speaking by rote – automatically. 'I'd better get out of here.' The transformation from Kentish Town to Holland Park was too much. He wasn't making the class shifts any more. He took a grape for emergency energy and stood up.

At that moment, Billy Cox's first cousin walked across to the table and apologized to Billy for being late, then dared to raise her eyes to Lucifer. Penny stared at him fully for almost a minute. She became radiant. She was transformed. Any light he had left, she absorbed. 'I'm so glad I found you', she said. 'Although these days you're everywhere. Especially on walls.'

The men had remained standing and agreed later that they had never seen anything like that except in the cinema. All Lucifer had to do was get out of there, and the arrival of this foolishly-devoted female was clearly the way out. Using his headache as an excuse, he said he would get some air and have a quick talk with Penny. 'So great to see her. What a surprise.' And he took her arm and left the restaurant.

Once outside, she told him she knew who he was. Lucifer stumbled on into the dark. How much worse did this evening have to get? He removed his glasses and hailed a cab. She asked where they were going.

'You are going home.'

Forcefully, she dismissed the cab and took Lucifer's arm. 'Billy knew you at Eton. Lucien de Montmorency. Have you dropped out? Is that it? You were right, Huysmans was Charles. I feel blessed to have known you.'

Lucifer felt he was going mad. He would need her uncle next.

'I'm so glad you are a Montmorency and not Lucifer. Are you for good, as in approval of good, or simply saying that Lucifer is here forever?'

'I wouldn't ask that.' And he looked for another taxi. 'I would find someone right for you and forget me.' He had said that over the centuries. The message and the result never changed. She exploded with tears and he had to comfort her and so miss another taxi.

'I can't bear the loss', she told him. 'I've felt as though I couldn't go on these last few days. My uncle said you don't know loss.'

'Oh, but I do', he said quickly, energy returning. 'I'm surprised your uncle doesn't know me better. I have felt terrible loss.'

'Who is she?'

'Venus.'

At least it wasn't a woman. Relieved, she asked if he meant the planet.

'Yes, Venus. My true love. My home. I can never . . .' He was going to add, 'go back there'.

'Have you loved a woman?'

'I have love for children.'

'Why don't you teach them? Tell them your story. You are a teacher. My cousin Billy Cox says you're marvellous. Teach children about good . . .'

Lucifer said it was a good idea, but how could it become reality?

'I can arrange it.' She had cheered up completely. 'I'm so grateful my cousin told me he knew you. Why do you especially love children?'

'Because they have innocence. They are authentic. Their souls are beautiful. If things were different here, they would do marvellous things.'

'What's wrong with here?'

He laughed dryly. 'It could be hell.'

He finally got her into a taxi and agreed to think about the children's lessons. He barely had the energy to pad back along the dark streets to his boudoir.

2017

The Boudoir

Lucifer circled the abandoned warehouse with its worn-out warning signs – 'DANGER BUILDING UNSAFE' – and met the wind from the River Thames, fierce and unexpected. Edging himself along the wall, he reached the narrow wooden door which creaked before he even touched the lock. The door had always been a good guardian and knew its stuff, having once belonged to an 11th century Spanish church. Once inside the vast disused building, he moved anti-clockwise in the lowering light and climbed lopsided stairs, swaying with age from some forgotten time. Reaching the second floor, he turned expertly clockwise and walked, shoes clicking smartly, with a complete sense of the expected; as though taking a well-worn commuter journey. In fact, the corridor had always been difficult for Lucifer and a show of bravado was the best he could manage.

Forsaken offices, each side of what had once been a busy corridor, were in the old days well kept – dealing with essential matters – but now the doors, covered with other peoples' graffiti, some hanging open, showed wooden desks, sinking and broken. Windows, cracked or smashed, allowed the boisterous wind to lift long-forgotten naval and dockyard documents, whirling like freed spirits, defying gravity. In spite of his manufactured calm, he increased his pace and, from an office at the far end, a bird screeched and fluttered mistakenly into the corridor, in search of freedom. Here, as

Lucifer knew only too well, was the passage of trapped souls, waiting, in a terrible existence, to be spared and allowed the progression into light. Some unthinkable mistake in the karmic order had delayed their journey. Around the round building, his pace never changing, he reached the mock-Grecian arch and was in a lighter stretch of corridor. He breathed easier. There was nothing he couldn't handle here.

He stopped at a sleek black door, its intense black varnish rich with hypnotic depths. A private door, always closed, it belonged in a gambling joint in Atlantic City. Level with the lock was a sign − The Stone Cradle − in elegant, fine gold lettering. One touch on the door and all the lights and colours of this forgotten corridor came to life. A different dimension replaced the previous emptiness and opened up another reality: the sound of dance music from the 1920s, gaiety, laughter, the chink of glasses, fizz of Champagne, the shiver

of silk gowns and the tinkle of chandeliers. The corridor –
somewhere back in a preserved moment – didn't bother him
at all as he unlocked the glamorous door and a haze of light,
yellow and soft, escaped as the door opened just enough to
allow him entry.

The smell of fresh jasmine was overwhelming and he
leaned back against the door, eyes closed, and the lock
clicked satisfactorily. He breathed and took in the full
enchantment of the blossom but couldn't get enough of its
dangerously sweet delight. It pleased him more than any
opiate. Violin music started up and Lucifer was in another,
older, era, far from the unnerving jangle on the other side of
the door. The violinist stood in the far corner and Lucifer
stayed still to absorb the challenging music and jasmine
scent, and slowly he was restored.

The atmosphere of the boudoir only *seemed* calm. It was
always busy with energies, frenetic and at odds with each
other like weather conditions at cross-purposes before a
storm. The clocks from all ages ticked variously and some
with madly spinning minute hands took time backwards.
They were always worse when Lucien, as he liked to be called
in the boudoir, was present. He felt they were mocking him. It
was all about time. Dark burgundy-papered walls, on which
celebrated paintings were displayed, recently shared their
space with framed charts of sacred geometry, some marking
pathways to Venus. A portrait of Lucien, 1760, seemed to
look out at the present modern-day interloper with disdain.

Lucien moved Olav's chinchilla stole from the dressing-
table chair and lit the oil lamps. The chrysanthemums from
Proust, still provocative, lifted their floral heads and he saw
his appearance reflected in the shine of the jewellery box. His

skin was as yellow as that of ageing pages in the medieval *Sworn Book of Honorius*. He dabbed his face with water softened by white rose petals. Looking at his perfume bottles and flasks gave pleasure. Gathered through the ages, these essences, toilet waters and potions, some to ward off the plague, restored his senses. He was cheered up enough to examine his latest graffiti on the end wall. The cheating moon cut off from the sun – its true provider of light – turned green and consumptive; a falling moon, damaged and dented from a collision with an asteroid. That was his favourite. 'It cheated me', said Lucien. 'Took me for all I had and now keeps my reflection.' He took a crayon and wrote angrily across the dented moon: 'Condemned'. Lastly, there was a swollen moon, damaged, its light dying and sinking into space.

Then he noticed the Elysium fox at the window, trying to get in. It scraped at the tinted glass. 'I have a message for you', it whined. Lucien signalled for the violinist to play something else. 'Angel of the Morning'. The fox laughed. 'That shop-girl ballad. You're losing your taste.'

Lucien sang along with the violin music. 'Just call me Angel of the Morning.' The fox joined in, its voice rasping and discordant. 'Just touch my cheek before you leave. And if we're victims of the night, I won't be blinded by the light.' Lucien signalled for the violinist to stop and turned to the fox: 'You dumb vermin. You sing out of tune. You're no nightingale. You rodent! Go sing to the dustbins.'

'You're a bastard', said the fox.

'Too true', agreed Lucien. 'But I thought my mother was the Countess of Montmorency.'

'Of course. Who else could you think of', said the fox. 'A social climber like you. What gave birth to you is not from hereabouts.' Although the fox used its best wiles to get its own way, Lucien would not let him in and instead lay back on his chaise lounge and turned the pages of Proust. 'You don't ask me about my message.' Lucien ignored him and turned another page. 'It might be from Venus.' Lucien did not react. Only the change in his breathing showed the fox he'd got him. 'Better open the window. I've got a short memory with age and I might get it wrong.' Lucien resisted the trickery, had seen it all before, and turned to the violinist for a different tune. 'If you let me in I will trace your mother', said the fox in a purring tone. 'I divine the past by smell. You all carry the smell of your mother. I will track it back for you.'

'There was an early one, mistress to the King, Louis 16th. I hoped she was my mother because she seemed to care for me.'

'That one was a slut', and the fox licked its paws.

'I ruined it all', said Lucien thoughtfully. 'I used to pick up men to be her lovers.'

'Nothing wrong with that', said the fox.

'Three at a time?'

'It's cold out here', moaned the fox. When he still wasn't let in, he became vicious. 'You haven't got a mother. You were created. Not born.'

'I know all that', said Lucien languidly, turning a page. 'I just hoped it was otherwise. My best time was with Louis 16th. I was well looked after. And there was, for me, a kind of innocence because my body was that of a young boy and women loved me.'

'A gay young boy', said the fox.

Lucien, restless, sat up. 'It has to be Paris. Remember Proust writing about my last possible mother. The pinnacle of society. The most noble family. And Proust's conclusion, when the character Charles Swann has finished with his mistress.' Lucien recited from memory. 'To think that I have wasted years of my life; that I have longed for death, that the greatest love that I have ever known has been for a woman who did not please me, who was not of my style.'

'Sounds like you and me', said the fox yawning. 'You are better off in Spain. They think they understand you.'

'I love Charlie Huysmans. Nothing natural there. Connoisseur of decadence. Sound, smell, taste.' And he hurried over to his scent bottles and plunged his nose across them all and gasped in enough essence to feel ecstatic. And the violin soared and Lucien choked and passed out from the pure high. When he was brought back to his senses by the violinist fanning his face, the window was wide open to give oxygen and the fox had got in and was sitting on the chinchilla, reading Lucien's diary.

'He used senses as doorways to lost memories. That must be Proust.' The fox turned another page.

'I hate know-alls', and Lucien got up. 'Yes, it has to be France. The old days were better.' He looked in the long mirror, which gave no reflection. All he saw was an endless passage of time, going back mercilessly. He stayed upright, unblinking. 'This is beyond punishment. They didn't tell me I was going to hell.'

'Better than the Stone Cradle', said the fox. 'It's not yours. Take that sign off your door. It's called LUN and will come of itself to them who wait for it. It was on Mount Sin of the Sumerians, then Mount Sion and now the Pyrenees. The stone goes always north.'

'Where do you get this stuff?' said Lucien, irritated.

The fox polished its claws with soft French cream from the dressing table. 'I've been around. In this case, Venus.'

And then it was all gone and Lucifer left the empty warehouse, circling one way then the other, speeding downwards. He'd stayed too long. Outside, the sign swung in the wind above his head: 'CONDEMNED'. And he circled off and hit the streets again.

2017, LONDON

The Ritz

The Prof. did not feign surprise when he saw Lucifer coming out of the Wolsley accompanied by two women, the sort favoured by Billy Cox. Having enjoyed the Wolsley's celebrated high tea with a few flutes of Champagne Royal, they crossed laughing to the Ritz, where Lucifer put them promptly into a cab. He wasn't laughing when he saw the Prof. watching from the pavement. The Prof. sensed that Lucifer was considering making-off fast into the park, but seemed to lose faith in that impulse and politely, even smiling, approached amiably enough. 'I'm glad I've run into you', said Prof. 'With a little help from Billy Cox.'

'Nothing is coincidence anyway', said Lucifer.

The Prof. led the way into the Ritz and, seated comfortably in the lobby, chose his favourite dry martini and a freshly-squeezed fruit cocktail for Lucifer. 'Your signs proliferate across town more than an advertisement.'

'They are an advertisement. That's the point. It's hard work getting the wings right. I prefer the graffiti I did at the railway station in Marseilles. You could say I started it.'

The Prof. thought Lucifer looked pale and drawn, and asked if he spent all night doing graffiti, or if he got others to do it for him. Lucifer considered his answer and, knowing he couldn't explain his noticeable lack of life, said yes to both. He even sounded exhausted.

'My niece has an idea for you to teach children.'

'I like that.'

'I don't.' The Prof. was definite. 'Also, I am asking you not to see her again. Spare her.'

Lucifer was silenced. When he spoke he was almost broken with fatigue. 'Spare? That's a big word. I haven't come across that lately.' He took an untidy gulp of his drink.

'I have found some of her private writing.' The Prof. lifted a sheet from his briefcase and read the copied text. 'I will follow you into death. I will be there for you beyond my last dying day. I will exchange my life for one moment in your light. Your light brings me enchantment that I have never known but always looked for.' Prof. turned the sheet and read a scribbled note. 'I pray to you, Lord of the Morning Light.' He slid the sheet back into the briefcase.

'Yes, not the kind of thing an uncle wants to read', said Lucifer, thoughtfully. 'Luckily, I'm not a family man. I feel out of place, to be honest.'

'Lonely.'

'Isolated. It's all too much.' Then he pointed to the brief-case. 'I've heard it all before. I already mentioned I had a chat once with Jung.'

Prof. nodded. 'About?'

'Eternity.'

'What did he say?'

'What could he say? He's never experienced it.' Lucifer stood up and asked for his coat.

'I like your niece. So I won't see her again.'

And he walked out to the crowded pavement towards Piccadilly, heavy with loss, dying of heartache. He almost laughed. 'Any of these hurrying humans would think I was in this state because of one of them. It's for a state of being I

mourn, that they could never understand. A perfection distant from here. Divine Venus that no longer knows my name.'
He swerved into St James' church where the musicians played Palestrina. It was almost sublime and three tears fell from Lucifer's eyes.

Mornington Crescent

'What is Lucifer?'

The children did not know. They sat, too well behaved, in a semi circle: a dozen girls and boys, mixed races, over 8 years and under 12, provided by the string-pulling of Penny W. This, a progressive school in a fairly poor district, should present no problem, she wrote. She'd sent him a note and he replied by letter. They did not meet again.

Lucifer chose the story of the snake in the Garden of Eden and a small girl spoke up before he had finished and said it was in the Bible. All eyes were on her as she explained that the snake had encouraged the woman, Eve, to eat of the apple and her eyes were opened and she saw herself as she was. And what, Lucifer asked, was wrong with that?

'She may not go down with everybody', said the oldest boy. 'You have to put some makeup on that sort of thing. You can't just go around not knowing who you are. I live in a block in Somers Town. Do you know it?' Lucifer, he could see, did not know Somers Town. 'It's a rough neighbourhood. You don't go in there alone. You have to know just who you are there.'

Lucifer cut through what would turn into a streetwise bio, and asked the first girl if she had heard about the Garden in church. She had not. She knew it from a lesson in Religion at school. When encouraged, a few of the others had also heard of the Garden and would have spoken, but a younger boy, James from Trinidad – unsure if his rebelliousness would stay contained in the room – asked how long this was going to take. Lucifer asked why time was so important.

'Because I have to sit just waiting for time to pass.'

How Lucifer knew that feeling. 'Lucifer is outside time. He was an archangel. The highest. But on offering the couple in the Garden the ability to see themselves as they were, he was judged disobedient and thrown out.'

'Where is this place?' asked the oldest boy. 'Is it an orchard?'

James jumped up, fingers snapping. 'Of course I know Lucifer. "Take Me". Hit song. "Make me good. I'm misunderstood." And I love your wings. On that great graffiti.' And, rocking to and fro around the room, he sung Lucifer's song and the others, without a thought, jumped up and danced with him. He leapt onto a table; the others leapt on everything. The eldest boy beat out the rhythm with a broom handle. The children were wild and full of music and vibration and sound. The room had been electric enough to start with, just having Lucifer present. Now, it was beyond any teacher's nightmare. And Lucifer changed the song to 'Angel of the Morning'. Did they know it? They knew everything. And clapping, singing, wailing and dancing they delivered his choice of song. Two men, one a guard, the other the headmaster rushed in and shouted for all this to stop. And a pretty girl, delicate and pale, started crying and James put his arms around her and comforted her. 'Sweet Lily, don't be frightened.'

'So this is what happens when you bring in the Antichrist.'

And the Head grabbed hold of Lucifer and had enough hate to single-handedly throw him out. Once again, he hit the streets of North London.

'Those kids don't stand a chance.' Lucifer got to his feet, angry for them. 'That pompous, sick gravedigger will squeeze every drop of life from them. That lunatic tyrant and all the others that will follow, terrified of a high they can never have, will impose a conformity, fed by fear. Those kids, destined to be distracted by mindless machines, imbecilic war games, televised rubbish, will end up with all their wonderful gifts obsolete, their love of life deceased. They'll be drinkers, sugar fat, tabloid *Sun* readers and bloated internet slaves.' But James, consoling the girl tenderly, stayed in his thoughts. He had held sweet Lily with a closeness that puzzled Lucifer. And, he realized, it was quite alien to him, that skin-to-skin, soothing love. He liked it better when they were unruly.

The Pallisades

The Prof. spoke rarely, so the place was always packed out for him, with standing room only. 'The Cradle is a meteorite that crashed to earth, millions of years ago. It is one of the oldest stones on the planet. It is made of iron, rock, chondrules and another constituent still not identified.' He stood, referring to his notes, without any awkwardness. He'd just returned from the Cradle site in northern Spain and hadn't had time to digest the material. 'I was fortunate to see the stone and respect the guardians' request for privacy, so this time my camera was not my too-frequent companion. What is special about this stone? Before it crashed through the meteor belt it would have been the size of a double-decker bus. Now, it's shaped like a fruit dish and rocks side to side, large enough for a man to lie on, full length. The stone is concave from being worn by the bodies of millions of supplicants through the ages. They come to lie on this stone because its purpose is to heal.'

'Are there any other stones like this on the planet?' asked a male student, eagerly.

'I expect there are', said Prof. 'But I know only of a meteorite further north in Le Puy in France, which has an identical colour but has flaws across the top, not concave. It is well known for its healing properties, especially during the plague years. But the Cradle is more powerful and, over the centuries, people have lain here to give birth, to be healed and to die. It is an elegant stone, absolutely smooth, with holes along the side where nutrients contact the human body and are absorbed by the skin. And this was where Lucifer, when he sank to earth 5,000 years ago, was lain and nourished. According to legend, he was the Child of Light, his purpose to teach and raise man's level of spiritual consciousness and awareness to the etheric, so man became capable of spiritual experience. A woman from the East came to look after Lucifer, and there remains an effigy of an Oriental woman in a small church in the mountains which has puzzled people for centuries. What had an Oriental to do with the Celts and the later Catalans? The Child of Light is a teacher that walked from place to place, lifting consciousness. He was present at the building of the first Pyramid and was acquainted with Seshat, the goddess of writing, measuring and psychic seeing.

'A note on the Cradle area. It has always been a vast, uninhabited wild expanse and, there, the crater is visible where the meteorite fell. It is not welcoming to visitors. It's difficult to navigate, with strong mountain winds and a tricky terrain filled with dolmens, chromlechs, standing stones, ritual carvings and portals. The energy points here are powerful. There is a strong connection with Venus – with several temples to Venus on the coast and in the mountains. All told, it is too pressurized for comfort. Not a place to visit, let alone live, but the magnetism of the Cradle must have been powerful to bring so many supplicants. The tradition tells of ritual practices in a disused chapel nearby, and the Cradle was always just lying open for years until, more recently, when, knowing of its powers, some people tried to steal it.'

Prof. took another pause, not to reach his glass of water but to check newcomers crowding into the room. Lucifer was not there. He then said a little about Jean Cocteau, the French filmmaker, sometime in 1913 taking a piece of the Cradle base and giving the stone to the artist Nicholas Roerich, who was working on a Stravinsky ballet in Paris. It later became the capstone of the UN.

What were the rituals used by the supplicants and guardians at the Cradle site? The Prof. had been told they made a passage directly to Venus, and Lucifer was associated with this planet but was denied entry to take the role of Master because he was considered the cause of the Fall.

'He casts the Pentagram. He blinds with light. What is behind? The void? Lucifer is eternal, denied rebirth and death. Is he still amongst us? The Church views him as the dark entity, the Antichrist, but in Spain I was surprised to see he is celebrated by a centuries-old guild of Light, or Luz. The Celts knew him as Lug. Further south, in the Girona province, there are several references to the Being of Light, including a private church in St Lucia. Why am I in this?' He let his papers rest on the podium. 'I like hidden history, which is why I belong to this organization. I like mysteries. I am interested in Lucifer's habitat.'

He had expected Lucifer would come. There was so much he now wanted to ask this stranger. During the quick question-and-answer session, he saw the shadow slide along the outer passage floor, almost to the door. It hovered undecided. It moved back and was gone. He thought he heard the light footsteps. He was disappointed. He was sure he would come. He never came.

Kentish Town: Time Running Out

Lucifer looked for Ollie in MacDonald's and Mick the Tick and his gang were at the main table. They waved him in and made a space, a small one. He asked if they'd seen Ollie. Lucifer didn't like the food, never had. 'I'm a vegan.'

'What's that?' The Tick was prepared to be insulted. Then he turned to the serving boy he knew behind the counter. 'Get him a shake and the works and put it on my bill.' He turned to Lucifer. 'If you're broke, say so. We've all been there.'

And Lucifer wolfed down the Big Mac with fries. He was a man like any other.

He roamed the streets, the grey sky a lid, the air thick and polluted. Only the sound of bells cheered him up; they always had. Like him, they were eternal. He thought about the children. They were born of scarcity, poorly-made. How could they get by on just two dimensions? Good-bad, right-wrong, left-right. The dual planet. Two when it should be four or glorious sixteen. But they had something he didn't. He realized it was choice. And, because they were small beings, it was on a small scale. They're lucky. They choose good and die easy. It hadn't occurred to Lucifer before. 'I can see them in the way they see an ant or a cockroach. All they know is how to kill it.' He almost wept, and three tears fell from his eyes. It was always three these days. Depressed, he did what these beings did at the end of their tether. He rushed into a church.

He stood at the back and raised his voice to the distant altar. 'I've seen the Highest of the Highest. I knew God. I am a magnificent being. Towers are dedicated to me. Churches, gardens, music, obelisks – all mine. A guild exists in my name.'

A woman in prayer turned and told him to lower his voice. 'I am looking for God.'

'Then you are in the right place', she said.

The priest approached him, carefully.

'I need help', Lucifer said, before the man could speak. 'Do you know the rite of the pentagram? Why do people here believe Lucifer is the Antichrist? What do you know about Lucifer? You are a priest. You guide people. I am a teacher in need of an answer. Yet you have nothing to tell me.' So far the priest had not had a chance to say one word. 'I am Lucifer.'

'Of course you are.' The priest knew better than to disagree with the ideas of a mad man. And at that moment the altar caught fire. The blaze was immediate. Struck, without doubt, by lightning.

Afterwards, the priest wasn't entirely sure about the meeting with the man. He had seemed insubstantial.

Kentish Town Station

As Lucifer stumbled up the high street in the evening light, people bumped into him as though he didn't exist. Ollie leaned against the tube station wall and Lucifer was pleased to see him. 'Ollie, what are you doing, still living?'

'You know everything, Lucifer. Can you tell me how to make a grave, so I know where I'm going? Otherwise they'll burn me.'

'Couldn't do that. I don't know anything about death.'

'Then can you teach my boy music. You're good at that. Or those designs you make. Circles on circles.'

Lucifer said: 'What's in it for me?' Then he laughed. He said he'd teach the boy sacred geometry. But first he had to take Ollie to the right place. The best.

2017, SPAIN

The Stone Cradle

They got to northern Spain, but he had to carry his friend the last kilometres over the rough terrain and laid him on the Stone Cradle.

Lucifer sat on the nearby rock staring across at Venus, his hands reaching out in supplication. Without blinking, his vision stretched to a point where he could just see the marvellous sphere with the surrounding bands of divine rose-pink and red light. Hardly breathing, he found he could reach further and through the moving bands; the yellow-gold celestial ladders were visible, with beings climbing and descending in beautiful unison. Now he could hear those sounds accessible to him,

traversing this narrowing space – chimes and tinkling bells announcing the language of Venus. The towers and minarets of the worshipful stations were apparent in brilliant orange. Lucifer was joyous. He was in reach of his beloved soul state.

'You are the Lamplighter.' A bird hopped beside him. 'You are not the Light Carrier anymore.'

'Everyone knows I am.'

'You were', insisted the arrogant creature. 'Time takes time to go from one place to another. The Everyone you mention gets the facts millenniums later.'

Lucifer felt like stamping on the upstart and crushing it to death, but he knew, how he did, that the bird spoke the truth.

'I don't trust messages from birds', he said coldly. 'I prefer what rustling leaves tell me.'

The bird flew off and Lucifer saw that, during this useless exchange, Venus had become covered with cloud. He got up and moistened Ollie's lips with mountain water. 'Don't be frightened. You are going on the most marvellous journey you've ever known, so let go with joy. Spirits pass through the Cradle on their way to death and birth. Some come from the Great Bear Constellation. I am the Angel of the Morning. I am with you, Ollie.'

'No-one can hear you. Not even the dying.' Lucifer recognized that croaking sound and turned and saw the Elysium fox, high on a hill looking down. The sound of the fox caused chaos and even Venus looked distant. Again, Lucifer tried to adjust his gaze. 'I belong there. Even this earth, teeming with buffoons, knows that. They call me the Morning Star.'

The trees rustled and he waited for a message. 'I never trust birds because they will say anything. They're scared of me.' He thought about the children. They would never comprehend the scale of chance. They don't even know pure mathematics or recognize sacred geometry. They have lost their country ways. But they had that skin-to-skin contact and care one for the other. It was tender; the love of a mother, which he had never felt. It made him want to cry.

The fox jumped down beside him and sniffed his face. 'Leave those children where they are.'

'Since when do you read thoughts?'

'I don't. The warning is old. It is said that if you follow Lucifer, you touch a joy and power that is too much for you and not yours to have. Children in the Garden Of Eden? Again? Is that what you want?'

Lucifer didn't like that message. 'That's from a long time ago. Who told you that?'

'Venus. I can read signs.'

Lucifer got up and walked to the edge of the hill. There were his wings, lying in a heap, crumpled and dirt covered. He knelt and touched them. 'They last better than Olav's furs.' He raised his eyes higher and stared into his beloved sphere. It made him shiver. He said again his prayer of longing and waited, wringing his hands, looking at what he loved and could not reach. Again he was not accepted.

'You have to wait for it to reach for you', said the fox, softly. 'Be patient.'

The fox turned away to make the dying man's last moments bearable. Lucifer remembered Penny's final words and whispered them to Venus. 'I am glad you are in my world.'

THE END

Books to challenge **C** *your perception of reality*

A message from Clairview

We are an independent publishing company with a focus on cutting-edge, non-fiction books. Our innovative list covers current affairs and politics, health, the arts, history, science and spirituality. But regardless of subject, our books have a common link: they all question conventional thinking, dogmas and received wisdom.

Despite being a small company, our list features some big names, such as Booker Prize winner Ben Okri, literary giant Gore Vidal, world leader Mikhail Gorbachev, modern artist Joseph Beuys and natural childbirth pioneer Michel Odent.

So, check out our full catalogue online at
www.clairviewbooks.com
and join our emailing list for news on new titles.

office@clairviewbooks.com

CLAIRVIEW